This Stargirl book belongs to:

_____

_____

_____

For Isabella, with love

First published 2013 by Walker Books Ltd
87 Vauxhall Walk, London SE11 5HJ

2 4 6 8 10 9 7 5 3 1

Text © 2013 Vivian French
Illustrations © 2013 Jo Anne Davies

The right of Vivian French and Jo Anne Davies to be identified
as author and illustrator respectively of this work
has been asserted by them in accordance with the
Copyright, Designs and Patents Act 1988

This book has been typeset in StempelSchneidler

Printed and bound in Great Britain
by Clays Ltd, St Ives plc

British Library Cataloguing in Publication Data:
a catalogue record for this book is available from
the British Library

ISBN 978-1-4063-4528-5

www.walker.co.uk

Stargirl Academy

Olivia's
Twinkling Spell

VIVIAN FRENCH

WALKER
BOOKS

Stargirl Academy

Where magic makes a difference!

HEAD TEACHER
Fairy Mary McBee

DEPUTY HEAD
Miss Scritch

TEACHER
Fairy Fifibelle Lee

TEAM STARLIGHT

Lily

Madison

Sophie

Ava

Emma

Olivia

TEAM TWINSTAR

Melody

Jackson

Dear Stargirl,

Welcome to *Stargirl Academy*!

My name is Fairy Mary McBee and I'm delighted you're here. All my Stargirls are very special and I can tell that you are wonderful too.

We'll be learning how to use magic safely and efficiently to help anyone who is in trouble, but before we go any further I have a request. The Academy MUST be kept secret. This is VERY important...

So may I ask you to join our other Stargirls in making The Promise? Read it – say it out loud if you wish – then sign your name on the bottom line.

Thank you so much ... and well done!

Fairy Mary

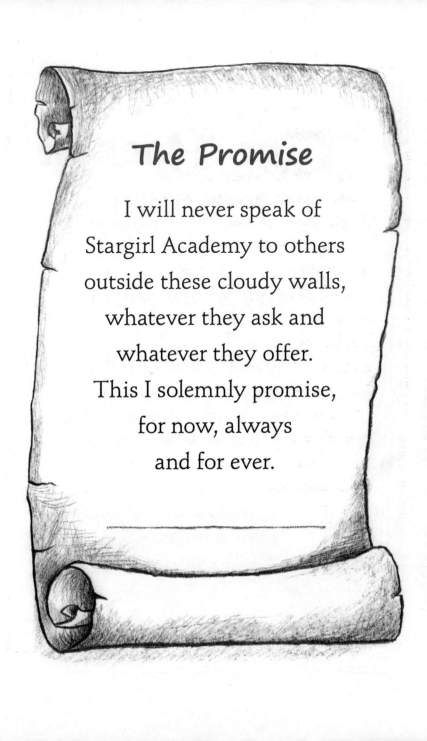

The Promise

I will never speak of
Stargirl Academy to others
outside these cloudy walls,
whatever they ask and
whatever they offer.
This I solemnly promise,
for now, always
and for ever.

The Book of Spells

by

Fairy Mary McBee

Head Teacher at

The Fairy Mary McBee
Academy for Stargirls

◆ ◆ ◆

A complete list of Spells can be obtained from the Academy.

Only the fully qualified need apply. Other applications

will be refused.

Twinkling Spells

Twinkling Spells are the most powerful
of all the Spells taught at the Academy, and
should be used with extreme caution. Any student
found using a Twinkling Spell incorrectly will be
asked to leave the Academy immediately.

The only Twinkling Spell available to students
at Stargirl Academy is the Choosing Spell, also
known as the Direction of Choice.

WARNING: though apparently simple, this spell
can have extremely far-reaching consequences.

Hello ... I'm very pleased to meet you. My name is Olivia Isabella Jones, and I think you might have met some of my friends at the Fairy Mary McBee Academy for Stargirls. I do hope you have, because they're wonderful!

Being chosen to be a Stargirl is the best thing that's ever happened to me. I'm on my own quite a lot, because Mum's always busy feeding my baby brother, or giving him baths, or changing his nappy. Sometimes Sophie comes round, or I go to her house, but she often has to look after her little brother Pete.

Sophie's a Stargirl too; I don't think

I'd have ever gone to the Academy if it wasn't for her. I'd never have dared to go through the huge front door, but she dragged me inside.

That's typical of Sophie! I'm quite shy, and I worry about things, but she doesn't. When the very first Tingle came and we disovered that it meant the Academy was floating nearby, and we'd be having lessons in spells and magic, Sophie was thrilled to pieces. I was a little bit excited – but I was worried as well. I thought my mum would be horribly anxious if she found I was missing ... but the head teacher, Fairy Mary McBee (she's SO lovely!), promised it would be all right. She told us that we'd get back home at exactly the same moment as we'd left, so nobody would ever know we'd been away. And I'm not

worried any more. I just look forward
to when the next Tingle arrives...

Love, Olivia xxx

Chapter One

I never thought a Tingle would come when I was away from home. Mum had dropped me off at Auntie June's house; she was taking my baby brother to the clinic, and Auntie June had asked me over to play with my cousin Hannah. I love Hannah; she's younger than I am, but we get on really well. She's got an older brother called Harry, but I don't think he likes me much. Hannah says he doesn't like any girls, and he's really mean to her when Auntie June isn't looking.

I was surprised that Hannah didn't open the door when I knocked. Normally she's hanging around waiting for me to arrive,

 15

but it was Auntie June who let me in. She gave me a hug, and then she said, "I'm SO pleased you're here, Olivia. Hannah's upstairs. She's meant to be doing her weekend homework, and she's having trouble with it." She shook her head. "She doesn't find school easy, you know. Not like you and Harry. I hoped she might do better when she changed schools.

She started brilliantly – she's well above average with her reading, apparently – but now they keep telling me she's not trying. I asked Harry to help her, but she wouldn't let him into her room. I'm sure she'll want to see you, though."

I nodded, and hurried up the stairs. I could hear Hannah crying before I'd even opened the door. "Hannah!" I called. "It's me! Can I come in?"

Harry popped out of his room. "She's just making a fuss," he said. "She's got to write a story and she says she can't. I told her she was stupid, so now she's crying. GIRLS!" And he disappeared again.

I thought, "BOYS!"

Hannah was lying on her bed, but she sat up as I came in, and I saw her eyes were puffy and red. "What is it?" I asked as I sat down close beside her.

Hannah sniffed. "Nothing," she said. "I was being silly."

There were loads of screwed-up bits of paper all over the floor. I picked one up, but as I began to straighten it out, Hannah snatched it from my hand. "Don't," she said. "It's rubbish!"

"Why?" I asked.

"Because it IS." Hannah tore it into tiny little bits. "It's rubbish rubbish rubbish."

I watched as she flung the bits in the waste-paper basket. "Can I help?"

"No." Hannah rubbed at her eyes. "It's fine."

It obviously wasn't, but I couldn't say anything. Instead I flicked over a couple of pages of the book on the bedside table. "Is this any good?"

 18

Hannah made a funny gulping noise. "I don't know. Mum bought it for me. She says the books I like are too babyish."

I was surprised. "My mum lets me read what I want."

"You're lucky." Hannah made a face. "But you're clever, and I'm not."

"Yes, you are," I told her. "Auntie June told me you were brilliant when you started at your new school."

Hannah's lip quivered, and I thought she was going to cry again, but she didn't. Instead she took the book and closed it before creeping very close to me. "If I tell you a secret," she whispered, "do you PROMISE you won't tell anyone? Not my mum, or your mum, and especially not Harry?"

I nodded. "I promise. Cross my heart and hope to die."

Hannah took a deep breath. "I can't read. Not properly. They gave me a test when I first got to Merrywood Juniors, and it was a book I knew by heart, so it was fine – and then we went on reading it in class, and I did OK. But then we

finished it, and I don't know the new one. I get the words wrong all the time and people laugh at me and call me names and Miss Fanshaw keeps saying I'm not trying and I DO try ... oh, Livvy, I really really REALLY do..." And then she was crying again, crying her eyes out—

And that was the moment when I got the Tingle. It was so sharp it made me jump, and I had to pretend I was coughing. I didn't know what to do. Poor Hannah was sobbing into her pillow, but I'd had the call to go to the Academy ... and then I thought that maybe that was a GOOD thing. If the Golden Wand pointed at me, I'd get to choose who to help. And if it didn't point at me, but at one of my friends instead, maybe I could tell them how unhappy Hannah was and I could persuade them that making things better for her would be a Very Good Deed.

PING! The Tingle came again, and it was even sharper than before. I patted Hannah's back. "Don't cry, Hannah. I'll help you..."

"How?" Hannah rolled over and stared up at me. "Nobody can. Not ever."

"I will," I promised. "Wait here. I'm just going to get some tissues." I shot out of her room, down the corridor to the bathroom ... and when I opened the bathroom door I found myself in the hallway of Stargirl Academy.

Chapter Two

Even though I knew I'd get back to Hannah at exactly the same moment I'd left her, I couldn't help wondering, "What if I don't?"

"You look as if you're worrying about something, Olivia." It was Miss Scritch, the deputy head. She was standing watching me, and although she can be scary, this time she was looking quite friendly.

"Oh!" I said. "My cousin's ever so unhappy. I've left her crying in her bedroom, and I was thinking, 'What if I'm late back?'"

"You won't be." Miss Scritch was

reassuringly firm. "Now, hurry along to the workroom. We've a lot to do. Remember, this could be the day when you win your final star!"

My heart leapt. Miss Scritch was right. Fairy Mary McBee, our head teacher, gave us our Stargirl necklaces on the very first day we met her, and they're magical.

REALLY magical! If we need to be invisible we tap them, and guess what? We can't be seen by ANYONE except each other and our teachers. And there's something else; something VERY secret and special. The school crest is on the pendant – six sparkly stars and two crossed wands – and each time we do a good deed, one of the stars lights up. All of us in Team Starlight have five shining stars now; one more and we'll be true Stargirls. It was SO exciting I could hardly bear to think about it! I ran the last few steps to the workroom, and rushed through the door.

My friends were sitting together at one end of the table. Melody and Jackson, Team Twinstar, were by themselves at the other end. They were looking gloomy, probably because they only have four stars each.

They aren't always terribly nice; and if I'm honest, I'm a bit scared of them, because I know they think I'm silly.

As I came in, Melody looked up at me. "Little Miss Scaredy Pants, you're

late," she drawled. "Did you have to go the long way round? Was there a nasty big spider on your doorstep?"

I knew at once that Fairy Mary McBee wasn't in the room. Melody would never have dared to say anything like that if she were. I pretended I hadn't heard her, and went to sit by Sophie.

Miss Scritch followed me in, but she didn't make any comment. Instead she clapped her hands, and at once there was the sound of music. It was lovely – very calm and soothing. I could feel myself relaxing.

Madison gave a huge sigh. "That's SO beautiful, Miss Scritch! How did you do it?"

Miss Scritch almost smiled. "It comes with being a Fairy Godmother," she said.

 27

"When you're a fully qualified Stargirl, you'll be able to do it too."

We looked at each other in excitement, and Lily whispered, "Jeepers creepers! That's AMAZING!"

"You haven't got your last stars yet," Jackson reminded us.

"And you might mess up your mission today," Melody added. She sounded as if she wouldn't mind very much if we did.

Miss Scritch gave her a chilly look. "Fairy Mary and I believe that Stargirls should be generous in spirit as well as in deed," she said.

Melody didn't answer, but I saw her give the tiniest of shrugs.

Ava was looking around the workroom. The cupboards were bulging, just as always, and the shelves were still heaped

high with books and bottles and jars full of the strangest things. I've never wanted to look too closely. Sophie once told me she thought she'd seen a jar labelled *Spiders' Breath*, and I really REALLY hate anything to do with spiders.

"I thought there was something missing," Ava said thoughtfully. "The Golden Wand's not here. It's usually hanging on the wall – does that mean we can't have the Spin today?"

Miss Scritch shook her head. "Fairy Mary's taken it next door. She'll be back any minute now."

Even as Miss Scritch was speaking, the door from the sitting-room opened and Fairy Mary McBee came bustling in. I was pleased to see she was carrying the Golden Wand, but a moment later I forgot all about it. Fairy Mary was followed by the tallest, thinnest, spindliest woman I've ever seen! She was SO tall that she had to fold herself up to get through the door, and even when she sat down next to Fairy Mary her head wasn't too far from the ceiling.

"This," Fairy Mary told us as we tried not to stare, "is my sister, Fairy Prim McBee, one of the finest Fairy God-mothers you will ever meet." And she beamed at her sister.

Behind me there was a muffled snort, followed by an explosion of smothered giggles. Melody and Jackson were collapsed over the table, spluttering with laughter. They saw us turn to look at them, and Melody did her best to stop, but she couldn't.

"I'm sorry!" she gasped. "But it's really funny! Fairy Prim's so incredibly tall and thin and Fairy Mary's—"

"Be silent, Melody!" Miss Scritch sounded SO angry that my stomach tied itself up into knots. "How COULD you be so rude!"

There was a terrible frozen silence ... and then Fairy Prim began to laugh.

Chapter Three

I'd never heard anyone laugh like Fairy Prim. She was so loud the windows rattled and three jars fell off the shelves and crashed to the floor.

"Dear girl," Fairy Prim boomed, her voice as loud as a foghorn, "you're quite right! We're ridiculous! QUITE ridiculous! We're like a knife and a spoon – always have been." She gave Fairy Mary a fond smile. "She's the dumpling and I'm spaghetti! She's the zero and I'm the number one. And when we're together, we look like the number ten!"

By now we were all laughing – well, all except Miss Scritch. She was still looking

 33

frosty. She made a tutting noise and clicked her fingers at the bits of broken glass and scattered herbs on the floor. At once they swirled into the air and put themselves together again, and the three jars flew back to their shelf.

"WOW!" Madison gave an admiring gasp. "That's super efficient!"

"It certainly is," Fairy Prim agreed, and she waved her hand at the shelves. There was a strange shimmer in the air, then the bottles and jars and books began to shiver and shake before hopping up and down so fast they were a multicoloured blur. Seconds later, they'd arranged themselves into the neatest rows, each jar and bottle labelled, and the books in order of size. "Mary's always been untidy," she boomed. "She was DREADFUL as a

child! Couldn't find my way across our bedroom for the mess—"

"Thank you, Prim darling," Fairy Mary interrupted. "Shall we save the memories for later?" She gave the rows of bottles a thoughtful glance. "You may be tidy, but your spelling is still appalling."

Fairy Mary was right. From where I was sitting, I could read some of the labels. *Cats Wisskers. Mushroom Storks. Spidders' Breth...*

Fairy Prim gave a loud bark of laughter. "Spelling? Who cares about spelling! I'm sure Miss Scritch can sort it out with a wave of her wand." She caught my eye, and gave me the most enormous wink. "Or Olivia could do it. She's a wonder at spelling!"

I stared at her. How did she know?

"I know all about you girls!" Fairy Prim spread her arms wide as if to hug us all. "Madison. Sophie. Ava. Lily. Emma ... and we must never forget Melody and Jackson!" Melody and Jackson shifted in their chairs and I saw them scowl, but Fairy Prim took no notice. She went on, "Two oddities, just like me. Sometimes the most interesting characters, I'd say ... though I would, wouldn't I? But you two have only four stars shining on your

magic necklaces, while Team Starlight
have five – so make sure you don't let me
down today." And she beamed at the two
of them. To my amazement, they smiled
back.

Fairy Prim nodded. "Good. Now, let's
begin." She fished in her pocket, pulled
out a little silver wand and waved it in
the air. At once the room was full of the
tiniest twinkling stars, and Fairy Prim's
dress was covered in silvery sparkles.

"Jeepers creepers," Lily whispered.

"Magic is a wonderful thing, Lily," Fairy Prim agreed. "And the spell I'm about to share with you is a Twinkling Spell, so we need twinkles to set the scene." She paused. "Do feel free to applaud."

Madison, Sophie and I began clapping, and Lily, Emma, Ava and Melody joined in.

Jackson gave Fairy Prim a thumbs up, but she was looking puzzled. "How is

making things twinkle going to help anyone?" she asked.

Fairy Mary McBee leant forward. "Twinkling Spells are the hardest level of spell, Jackson dear ... and there are several different Twinkling Spells."

"Oh yes." Jackson's face cleared. "I remember now. Like learning to float things was actually a Shimmering Spell."

"The spell you'll learn today is the Choosing Spell," Fairy Prim told her. "If someone is trying to make up their mind, you'll be able to influence them ... and that is a very powerful spell indeed!"

"Wow!" Melody sat up, her eyes shining. "So I could get my mum to give me lots more pocket money?"

"Absolutely not." For the first time, Fairy Prim stopped smiling. "That is entirely

39

the wrong kind of application. In fact, the spell might reverse, and the results could be most unfortunate."

Emma put up her hand. "Please, what does that mean?"

"It means," Miss Scritch said sharply, "that the spell goes in the opposite direction. If Melody's mother was choosing between keeping Melody's pocket money the same, or giving her more, she would be making a choice. If Melody was foolish enough to use the Choosing Spell to persuade her mother to increase her allowance, it's more than likely that she would end up with nothing ... and it might well be that her mother would lose her money too. Every penny!"

Chapter Four

We all looked at each other.

"Oh dear," Madison said. "The Choosing Spell does sound tricky..."

"There's no problem if you're careful." Fairy Prim was smiling again.

Miss Scritch folded her arms. "Fairy Mary! Are you quite sure our Stargirls are ready for this?" She sounded as if she was certain that we weren't, but I could tell by Fairy Mary's frown that she didn't agree.

"I do think they're ready, Miss Scritch," she said. "I have every faith in them. Please go on, Prim dear."

Fairy Prim stood up, and began to walk

41

round the table. "Repeat after me:

I choose to use the Choosing Spell,

I choose it now, to use it well..."

We repeated the words, and when we knew them by heart Fairy Prim nodded. "Good. When you need the spell, say the words, point with your star finger and think of the choice you want the person to make. And I warn you, you'll have to think very hard!"

"Do we get to practise?" Ava asked.

Fairy Prim put her silver wand in her pocket and rubbed her nose thoughtfully. "I think we could. What do you think, Mary?"

"Why don't we have our morning snack first," Fairy Mary suggested. "We can practise afterwards."

"Excellent!" Fairy Prim whipped her

wand back out and waved it madly. "Cake and buns! My favourite kind of spell! What would you like, Miss Scritch?"

Miss Scritch had been looking extremely frosty, but now she thawed a little. "Thank you, Fairy Prim. Ahem. I have to confess that cucumber sandwiches are a favourite of mine."

"Cucumber? Consider it done!" Fairy Prim beamed as an enormous plate of cucumber sandwiches floated down onto the table. "I like banana and peanut butter, myself. And chocolate cake. And iced buns, of course. And—" she said, drawing a couple of zigzags in the air with her wand— "I know what my sister likes. Strawberries and cream!"

I don't think I'd ever seen such an enormous bowl of strawberries, and every single one was red and juicy. The jug of thick yellow cream was huge as well. I gave Fairy Mary a sideways glance, and I saw that she was looking pleased ... but also worried.

"Really, Prim," she said. "If we eat all this we'll need to lie down and sleep for a week!"

"Sleeping? Ha HA!" Fairy Prim's shout of laughter shook the room, and a flurry of dry leaves floated down from the bunches of herbs hanging from the ceiling. Fairy Prim blew them away with a flick of her wand. "There'll be no time for sleeping. We've a full programme today! We'll practise the spell, then it'll be time for the Spin, and then we'll go adventuring! We're going to have a ball, I can tell you."

Miss Scritch put down her sandwich and gave a dry little cough. "Excuse me, Fairy Prim, but the girls are expected to undertake their Stargirl missions on their own. Fairy Mary and I do not ever accompany them." She coughed again. "Fairy Fifibelle Lee, another member of the Academy, has, from time to time, chosen to be an invisible presence – but she has not, as far as I am aware, ever interfered."

Fairy Prim swung round. For a moment I wondered if she was offended, but the next minute she was laughing again. "Don't worry, Miss Scritch. I'll make sure I don't interfere. And the girls will never know I'm there." She shook her wand, tiny stars shimmered and then she was gone. "Is this invisible enough?" her voice asked, and the bowl of strawberries sailed across the table as if it was flying. "Can you see me, Miss Scritch?"

Miss Scritch hesitated, then smiled an unwilling little smile. "No," she admitted. "Even I can't see you, Fairy Prim."

Fairy Mary patted something in the air. "Prim was always top of the class when we were learning invisibility spells," she said proudly. "Do come back, Prim dear. It's so difficult to have a conversation with someone you can't see."

There was another flurry of stars, and Fairy Prim reappeared. "Thank you, Mary, for those kind words. Now, who would like some strawberries?"

Chapter Five

Fairy Mary was right. By the time we'd finished the delicious cake and sandwiches and strawberries, we did feel sleepy – at least, I did. I found myself yawning as Fairy Mary floated the dirty cups and plates away, but a chilly look from Miss Scritch woke me up.

Fairy Prim settled herself at the top of the table. "Now, shall we practise our new spell?" She pulled a pack of cards out of her bag and spread them over the table with a flourish. They weren't at all like the cards Hannah and I use when we're playing snap; they had the strangest pictures – cats and pumpkins, flowers

and castles, and all sorts of other things.

"Look!" Madison said. "There's a picture of a pair of glass slippers! And a spinning wheel! Oh, and what a FANTASTIC ballgown! Are they special cards for Fairy Godmothers?"

"Of course," Fairy Prim said. "It's sometimes helpful to remind ourselves what a Fairy Godmother can do."

I wondered if she was joking, but I didn't like to ask. I looked at the cards instead; some of the pictures seemed to be moving. I was almost certain that a big fat cat had winked at me, but when I looked more closely it had its eyes closed.

"Ava, Emma, Jackson and Lily," Fairy Prim said, "please leave the room. When you come back, Madison, Sophie, Olivia and Melody will use the spell to persuade you to choose the card they have selected."

I began to feel nervous as I looked at my star finger. On our very first day at Stargirl Academy, Fairy Mary McBee had floated stars round us, and a tiny one had stayed glowing on the tip of my littlest finger. "That's your star finger," Fairy Fifibelle Lee had told me. "All of you Stargirls will have one. You'll use it when you do magic ... but be careful. If you use it for the wrong kind of magic it'll disappear."

I sighed. My tiny star was glowing, but very faintly. Would I be able to make the spell work? Sophie gave me an encouraging smile. "Don't worry," she whispered. "You'll be fine!"

Fairy Prim was looking at Madison. "Which card will you choose for Ava?" she asked.

Madison studied the cards. "I think ... that castle. The one with the flags."

Fairy Prim nodded, and wrote something down in a little glittery notebook. I hadn't seen her get it out of her bag, so it must have appeared by magic.

Sophie picked a frog for Emma, and I chose a pink fluffy kitten for Jackson, because I knew she thought things like that were silly – and I really did want to see if I could make the spell work.

Miss Scritch surprised me by giving me an approving nod. "An excellent choice, Olivia."

Melody sniffed. "You'll never get Jackson to choose that. She hates fluffy stuff. I'm going to take the spinning wheel for Lily. It looks boring."

"Splendid!" Fairy Prim closed her notebook with a snap. "Sophie, dear, please ask the others to come back one at a time."

Jackson was the first. She began heading round the table to her place next to Melody, but Fairy Prim stopped her. "You're fine where you are," she said. "Perhaps you'd look at the cards while Olivia tries the spell."

I couldn't believe that Fairy Prim had asked me first! I could feel myself shaking as I tried to remember the words. *"I choose to use the Choosing Spell,"* I whispered, *"I choose it now, to use it well..."* I pointed my star finger at Jackson, and I thought of the pink fluffy kitten card just as hard as ever I could. "Pink fluffy kitten!" I thought. "Oh, PLEASE choose the pink fluffy kitten!"

Jackson was looking down at the cards, frowning. "I can't feel myself wanting to choose any of them," she said, and my heart sank. "I'd say Olivia isn't trying hard enough."

I shut my eyes, and tried even harder. I could actually see the picture inside my head ... but a little voice somewhere deep inside was telling me that it wasn't any good. I wouldn't be able to do it.

"Ta da!"

I opened my eyes to see Jackson waving a card in the air – and it was the pink kitten!

I gave a huge gasp of astonishment, and Jackson grinned at me in a superior kind of way. "You see? You couldn't do it. You'd NEVER think I'd want a fluffy wuffy kitty."

I was so surprised I couldn't speak. It was Fairy Mary who said, "Well done, Olivia!"

"What?" Jackson stared at her. "What's she done?"

"Olivia has given us a wonderful demonstration of the Choosing Spell," Fairy Prim told her. "That was the card she chose for you. There's just one thing missing." She waved her hand, and the tiniest twinkling stars floated gently down from the ceiling.

Miss Scritch raised her eyebrows. "Aren't those a little late?"

Fairy Prim chuckled. "You've caught me out, Miss Scritch. I interfered. I delayed the twinkles so Jackson wouldn't suspect anything."

"Hmph." Jackson was looking puzzled.

"That's so weird! It felt EXACTLY as if I'd made up my own mind!"

"That," Fairy Prim said, "is why this is such a dangerous spell."

Chapter Six

I was hugely relieved that I'd managed to get the spell right. Madison and Ava were successful too, but Emma didn't choose Sophie's frog. Instead, she picked up a picture of a large green cabbage.

Fairy Prim smiled. "Don't be down-hearted, Sophie. You're nearly there. Now, let's swap round."

I'd forgotten that I'd have to have a turn the other way. As Madison, Melody, Sophie and I left the workroom, I saw Jackson looking closely at the cards. "Ooops," I thought, and I wondered what it would be like to have a spell put on me.

I didn't have to wait long to find out. I

 58

was the first to be called back, and Fairy Prim asked me to study the cards while Jackson said the magic words. I waited for a moment or two to see if any particular picture attracted my attention, but none of them stood out.

"Go on, Olivia! Pick a card!" Jackson said.

"OK," I said. I'd liked the picture of the cheerful orange pumpkin when Fairy Prim spread the cards on the table, so I picked up that one.

But Jackson frowned. "That's not the right one," she said. "It's not even the right colour!"

"Perhaps," Fairy Mary said quietly, "you were wanting Olivia to choose your card for the wrong reasons, Jackson. Perhaps you wanted to show her that you're as clever as she is, rather than finding out if you could make the spell work."

Jackson made a snorting noise. "No! I certainly didn't—" she began, but then she saw Fairy Prim looking at her. "Um," she said. "Maybe you're right. Just a bit."

Fairy Prim clapped her hands. "Well done, Jackson! For admitting that, you can have another turn. But think about the spell. Don't worry about anything else."

Jackson murmured the words again, and this time it was strange. A rather dull picture of a horse suddenly caught my eye, and before I knew what I was doing it was in my hand – and Jackson was punching the air. "I did it!" she crowed, and I couldn't help giving her a thumbs up in return.

Fairy Prim cheered so loudly that Madison, Sophie and Melody came running in to see what was going on.

Miss Scritch made a tut-tutting noise. "Rather too much excitement, if I may say so." She pulled a small gold watch from her pocket, and frowned at it. "We should be moving on to the Spin very soon."

"We'll be there in no time at all," Fairy Prim promised. "But everyone must try the spell."

While the others had their go, I thought about what had happened. Just like Jackson, I hadn't felt as if anyone was trying to persuade me to do anything, and I began to see why Fairy Prim had described the spell as dangerous. It would be terrible to change someone's mind for the wrong reasons ... but maybe the spell couldn't do that? And for some reason that made me think of Auntie June trying to make Hannah read a book she didn't feel ready for. Was that right?

I gave up trying to make sense of it all, and discovered that while I'd been thinking Fairy Mary had put the Golden Wand in the middle of the table and was getting ready for the Spin. The room was already beginning to darken, and the wand had begun to glow.

"Mary, dear!" Fairy Prim obviously thought she was whispering, but she was still VERY loud. "It's a long time since I've done this. Am I right in thinking the wand will choose what happens for the rest of today?"

Fairy Mary nodded. "When the wand stops spinning, it will point at today's Stargirl. She will choose who she would like to help, and then the girls will plan how this can best be done." Fairy Mary's voice always softened when it was time for the Spin, and she already sounded mysterious and magical. "And now, let us begin..." She touched the wand, and six golden stars floated up and up until they were lost in the darkness. The wand began to spin, round and round and round, and a gentle humming filled the room.

"Hannah," I thought dreamily. "It would be so wonderful if I could help her..."

"Spin, spin, spin," Fairy Mary murmured. "Who will choose? Who will it be? Whose destiny will change today? Spin, wand, spin."

The wand spun on and on, and the humming grew more and more intense. My head was filled with the sound, and it made me feel strange and drifty. My eyelids grew heavy, and I rested my head on my hands—

SNAP!

The wand stopped with a jerk, and bright sunlight flooded the workroom. I blinked, and rubbed my eyes. For a moment I wondered if I'd actually fallen asleep; Sophie was shaking my arm as if

she was waking me up, but then I realised
she was trying to attract my attention.

"Olivia! Look! The wand's pointing at
you!"

Sophie was right. The wand *was* pointing
at me, and Fairy Prim had already jumped
up from her chair and was towering over us.
"Olivia dear, do tell! Where are we going?"

Chapter Seven

I still felt as if I might be dreaming. I rubbed my eyes again, and looked around. Everyone was watching me expectantly, even Melody and Jackson.

"I'm sorry," I said. "The Spin made me feel really weird..."

"Come on," Jackson said. "Hurry up! If you don't know who to help, I can think of HUNDREDS of people!"

"But I do know," I told her. "I want to help my cousin Hannah. She's really unhappy."

"Go on!" Melody was impatient. "Why's she unhappy?"

I hesitated, and looked at Fairy Mary.

"Hannah made me promise not to tell anyone what was wrong."

"Then you must respect her wishes," Fairy Mary said. "I'm sure you'll think of a way to help her without breaking your promise."

Miss Scritch gave me a little nod. "That's right." She stood back from the table and took Fairy Prim's arm in a firm grip. "We'll leave you to discuss your plans. Fairy Prim, I'm sure you and Fairy Mary would like a nice cosy chat in the sitting-room. The fire's lit, and the old Fairy Godmothers are longing to see you again. They've been leaning out of their portraits all morning."

For a moment Fairy Prim hesitated, but then she shook her head.

"Good try, Miss Scritch!" she boomed.

"But I want to see these girls in action." She gave our deputy head such a hearty slap on the back that she nearly fell over. "I didn't come all this way just to see Mary, you know." She saw Miss Scritch's disapproving expression, and beamed at her. "But I promise. No interfering! I'll be as quiet as a mouse. And a whole lot more invisible!" And at once she faded away, and there was not the slightest sign that she was in the room.

"Really!" Miss Scritch snapped.

But Fairy Mary smiled. "Don't worry," she said. "She knows the rules. Let's conjure up a pot of tea. And I'm sure my poor old dog would love a biscuit…" And, still talking, Fairy Mary led Miss Scritch out of the room.

"Hmph!" Melody folded her arms. "So

 68

how exactly are we going to help your cousin when you won't even tell us what's wrong with her, Olivia?"

I didn't answer straight away. An idea was slowly making itself clear in my mind. "I think," I said, "we need to see what happens to Hannah when she's at school. That's when things go wrong."

"Is she being bullied?" Ava asked. "That's horrible."

Jackson looked interested. "We can soon sort that one out. Look what we did to Lily's mean old aunt."

"She's not mean any more," Lily said.

Jackson grinned. "The power of the Stargirls! So where do we go, Olivia?"

"Hang on a minute." Madison waved her spectacles at me. "It's Saturday today. No school."

I'd just had the same thought. "Oh dear," I said.

"Ahem." It was Fairy Prim's voice, coming from the ceiling. "Time travel, my dears."

"What?" We stared upwards, and a couple of old dried leaves floated down.

"Time travel. You have the use of a Travelling Tower, I believe? Well, there's more than one way to travel." Fairy Prim chuckled loudly. "There's up and down, and to and fro ... but there's also before and after."

"Can we really do that?" Emma asked, her eyes shining with excitement.

I could feel a nasty cold feeling in my stomach. Time travel! Would we be safe? What if we couldn't get back?

"Sounds like a brilliant idea to me."

Sophie was excited too. "Can we go backwards AND forwards in time?"

I think Fairy Prim must have shaken her head, because several bunches of herbs swung wildly to and fro. "Oops!" she said as she suddenly materialised, leaves in her hair and a large dusty smudge on her nose. "There. That's better. Now you

can see me. And the answer, Sophie, is no. Only backwards, and only for a very short period of time."

"Jeepers creepers!" Lily clapped her hands. "Will we be able to do that on our own when we're proper Stargirls?"

"You'd need to use the Travelling Tower," Fairy Prim told her.

I was feeling worse and worse. "Are you sure it's all right?" Everyone turned to look at me in surprise, and I knew I was blushing. "I mean, we haven't ever done anything like that before..." My voice trailed away. I could see from the way Melody and Jackson were staring that they thought I was completely pathetic.

Sophie leant over and gave me a hug. "It'll be exciting, Olivia! You said you wanted to see what happens when

Hannah's at school, didn't you? Well, if we go back to yesterday you can do that!"

"Yes," I said. Sophie was right, but I still felt anxious. "What will Fairy Mary say? We've never time-travelled before."

"You've never had five shining stars on your magic necklace before." Fairy Prim gave me a reassuring smile. "You're very nearly a proper Stargirl, Olivia."

"And surely someone who's nearly a proper Stargirl should be brave. Isn't that right, Fairy Prim?" I knew Jackson was sneering at me, even though she was smiling, and I suddenly thought of Harry sneering at Hannah.

I took a deep breath. "I didn't say I wouldn't try," I said. "What do we have to do, Fairy Prim?"

Fairy Prim strode towards the door,

and beckoned us to follow. "Onwards and upwards," she said.

Madison hurried to join her. "Upwards? How far up will we go, Fairy Prim?"

My stomach gave a horrible lurch. Would we have to fly? But Fairy Prim gave her big booming laugh. "Only up to the Travelling Tower," she said, and she led the way out of the workroom.

Chapter Eight

As we walked along the corridor that led to the Travelling Tower, I tried to think of a plan to help Hannah. If we went backwards in time we'd be able to see what happened to her when she was at school. But what then? I was pretty sure we wouldn't be able to help her learn to read by magic. It didn't work like that. So what *would* we be able to do?

"What are you worrying about now, Olivia?" Sophie can always tell when I'm worrying. She says my face screws up.

"Hannah," I said with a sigh.

Sophie squeezed my hand. "It'll be OK. You'll see."

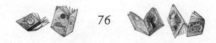

She was kind to say so, but I didn't feel much better – and a moment later we arrived at the Travelling Tower.

Fairy Prim looked at the glass walls with interest. "Mary told me about this," she said. "So much more modern than in my day. We always had to make our own way to the castles or palaces or orphanages where people needed help. Now, how does it work?"

Ava pointed to the switches and levers. "This lever takes us up," she explained, "and this one takes us down."

"Let's get going, then." Fairy Prim looked in my direction. "What school does your cousin go to, Olivia?"

"Merrywood Juniors," I said. "It's on Grisewood Drive."

Fairy Prim nodded. "And when would

be a good time to arrive, do you think?"

I wasn't sure what she meant, but Emma did. "The beginning of breaktime," she said firmly. "We can see what happens in the playground. That's one of the times when bullies pick on people."

"I see." Fairy Prim nodded again. "Then let us aim for 10.30am, yesterday morning." And she pulled out her wand and waved it in the air.

At once there was a sickening jolt as the Travelling Tower pulled away from the walls of Stargirl Academy, followed by a series of horrible lurches. Madison and Lily fell over, and I only saved myself by hanging on to the safety rail. If I'd had any breath left I'd have screamed. Sophie clung to my arm, and Emma, Melody, Ava and Jackson tumbled into a corner in a heap.

"Whoops-a-daisy!" Fairy Prim was quite unbothered. "Perhaps you should all sit down, my dears. This might be rocky to begin with. It'll take me a moment to get used to the steering."

"Stop! STOP!" Lily sounded almost as scared as I was. "Fairy Prim! We don't do it like this! We always float to where we need to go!"

"That's right!" Melody's voice was shrill. "The academy sits on a cloud—

79

OH!" She was interrupted by another lurch. "That's why it was called Cloudy Towers!"

Fairy Prim gave a casual shrug. "DO sit down, Melody dear. Of course I know about Cloudy Towers. I learnt everything I know here, didn't I? But we can't take the Academy back in time. It'd fall apart for sure. Now, hang on to your hats, and here we go!"

I think I'll always remember what happened next, even though Fairy Prim said later that she'd used the Forgetting Spell so we wouldn't have nightmares. It was the most frightening thing that's EVER happened to me! The Travelling Tower began to turn over and over and over and we were shaken about inside like peppercorns in a pepper pot. I think

we all screamed. I know I did ... and I
rather think Fairy Prim did too – just once
or twice. Either that, or she was shouting
"WHOOOOOHOOOOOOO!"

It seemed to go on for ages and ages.
Sophie and I clung to each other as if we
were drowning. But then, all of a sudden,

everything was quiet. It took a long moment to realise we weren't moving any more.

Very carefully, after checking we were all in one piece, we sat up.

"Here we are, my dears!" Fairy Prim gave us a beaming smile. "I'm sorry about the ride, but that's time travel for you. Olivia, dear, are we in the right place?"

My legs felt like jelly as I stood up and made my way to look out ... and when I saw where we were, I had to rub my eyes

before I could believe what I was seeing. Fairy Prim had done it! We were floating above Hannah's school playground. Loads of children were running about beneath us, jumping and hopping, or chatting in little groups.

I peered down, trying to spot Hannah.

"Can you see your cousin?" Ava asked.

"No." I went on staring, but there was

no sign of Hannah anywhere.

"Maybe she didn't go to school yesterday!" Jackson was half-laughing, half-jeering. "Maybe we've all been shaken to bits for nothing."

I shook my head. "She definitely went."

"Could she have been kept in?" Madison came to stand beside me.

Fairy Prim reached up and opened one of the glass doors, and a babble of voices filled the Travelling Tower. "I suggest you go and see for yourselves. Is everyone wearing their necklace? Time to be invisible!" And she vanished so quickly it made me blink.

Sophie and I tapped our necklaces, and the magic happened, like it always does. We could just about see each other if we squinted hard, but nobody who wasn't a Stargirl would be able to tell that we were there. The rest of Team Starlight followed our example, and so did Melody and Jackson. If anybody had peered into the Travelling Tower they would have thought it was empty.

"Ava!" It was Fairy Prim's voice. "Take us down into the playground!"

Chapter Nine

I wasn't at all sure it was a good idea to take the Travelling Tower into the middle of a busy playground, but Fairy Prim must have waved her wand when I wasn't looking. We landed right beside the school entrance, and I heaved a sigh of relief as the glass door slid open. I knew the TT was invisible to everyone except us, but I didn't want one of the infants crashing into it by mistake.

"Which way to Hannah's classroom?" Sophie whispered in my ear.

"This way." I hoped I was right; I'd only been to the school once, when Mum and I had come to collect Hannah. I walked off as if I knew where I was going, and I could feel Sophie close beside me – but then I stopped. I'd had a scary thought. "Who's going to wait in the TT? What if something goes wrong?"

"It's OK. Didn't you hear Fairy Prim?" I could tell Lily was smiling by her voice. "She said, 'YOU go and see for yourselves' ... so she must be staying."

I remembered how Miss Scritch had told Fairy Prim not to interfere, so that made sense. All the same, I still felt nervous as I led the way through an open door and along a corridor. But then I saw a classroom with Miss Fanshaw's name on the door, and I knew that at least I'd found the right room.

"Here we are," I whispered. "Let's tiptoe inside and see if Hannah's there. Quiet as mice!"

"We can't all go in," Madison pointed out. "Eight of us will be too many. I'll wait out here with Lily."

"Me too," said Emma, and I could just see Jackson nod.

"OK," I said. I slid inside – and there was Hannah, sitting all by herself in a corner, crying. Tears were rolling

down her cheeks and plopping onto the
pages of the book in front of her ... and
I COMPLETELY forgot I was invisible.
I rushed forward and hugged my poor
miserable cousin – and she let out a
terrified shriek, and leapt to her feet. I
was so surprised I staggered backwards

and knocked against a bookshelf – and it fell over, with the loudest crash ever. Books scattered in all directions, and the jar of pencils on top tumbled to the ground right in front of my horrified eyes. I tried to catch it, but all I did was knock it sideways into the radiator. The jar smashed into a thousand pieces, and pencils flew everywhere.

Hannah froze, her eyes wide. I felt sick.

"Quiet as mice, Olivia?" Melody whispered, and I knew she was laughing.

A teacher came running through the door. "HANNAH! Whatever's going on here?"

"I ... I don't know." Hannah was very pale. "Something touched me, and I jumped..."

"Something touched you?" It was clear

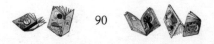

the teacher didn't believe her. "Really, Hannah! I leave you here to practise your reading, and you wreck the classroom! Just LOOK at what you've done! Books and glass everywhere! Go and report to Mrs Wheeler. I'll have to get this mess seen to before someone cuts themself."

"Yes, Miss Fanshaw." Hannah drooped

 91

away from her table, and made her way
slowly towards the door.

"Don't slouch!" Miss Fanshaw snapped,
and then she sighed. "If only you'd try,
Hannah, life would be so much easier for
you. You did so well when you first came
here."

"Yes, Miss Fanshaw." It sounded as
if Hannah had heard it all before. She
walked wearily out into the corridor, and
we followed her. My mind was whirling.
I'd made things a million times worse
for Hannah, and I had absolutely no idea
what to do next.

"It's her teacher who's bullying her!"
Ava breathed. "I TOLD you she was being
bullied! What should we do?"

"You could try hugging Miss Fanshaw!"
Melody suggested. "Hugging Hannah

certainly shook her up!"

Lily gave a snort. "Or we could float things around her head every time she's horrid."

"No." I was in a panic, but even so I couldn't agree with Ava. Miss Fanshaw wasn't nice, but I didn't think she was a bully. Something else was wrong, and I needed to find out what it was.

As we followed Hannah down the corridor two girls and a boy were coming in the other direction, and we had to flatten ourselves against the wall to let them pass. The girls gave Hannah a friendly wave, but the boy rolled his eyes and made a horrible face at her. "It's dumbo Hannah," he sneered. "Can't read, can't write, bet you wet the bed at night!"

"Shut up, Josh." One of the girls glared

at him. "Leave her alone! You're not that good at reading yourself."

"I'm better than her." Josh made an even more disgusting face. "She's thick as a stick!" And he ran on down the corridor, laughing.

The other girl groaned. "He's horrible. Ignore him, Hannah."

"Oh, thanks, Phoebe. Thanks, Sarah."

Hannah gave the two girls a weak smile.

At the other end of the corridor, there was a screech, followed by loud wailing. I swung round, and saw Josh clutching his head. "My ears!" he yelled. "A ghost's trying to pull my ears off!"

"Serves you right," Sarah said, and

she and Phoebe turned into Hannah's classroom without giving him another glance. I couldn't help wondering which

Stargirl had decided to teach him a lesson, but Hannah was almost out of sight and I had to run to catch her up.

As I hurried after her, Jackson chuckled in my ear.

"There's your bully, Olivia! He'll think twice before he calls Hannah names again!"

"Good," I said, but I still didn't think that solved the problem.

I found Hannah standing outside the head teacher's office.

A small boy came scuttling up carrying a note, and he grinned at her. "Hi," he said. "Is Mrs Wheeler in?"

"I don't know," Hannah told him. "I've only just got here." And she knocked on the door. As she did so, Phoebe and Sarah came towards us; when they saw Hannah, they didn't look quite as friendly as they had before.

"Miss Fanshaw says we can't use the classroom until the glass you broke has been cleaned up," Sarah told Hannah. "And we need to finish our project."

"I'm really sorry," Hannah apologised. "It was the weirdest accident – I still don't know how it happened."

Phoebe shrugged, then smiled. "It's OK. We didn't think you'd done it on purpose."

Hannah looked as if she was about to apologise again, but at that moment the head teacher's door opened and a tall elderly woman came out.

"Yes?" she said. "Who knocked?"

Hannah stepped forward, but before she could say a word the little boy wriggled

in front of her and held out his note.

"Please Mrs Wheeler, this is dead urgent from Mr Pole. Could you send a helper straight away, cos it's time for the Special Reading class and I ain't got nobody to help me!"

"You haven't got anybody, Vinnie," Mrs Wheeler corrected him, but she was smiling as she opened the note. "Ah! I see." She looked at Hannah, Phoebe and

Sarah. "I'm sure one of you three would be perfect..."

Hannah blushed. "Please, Mrs Wheeler, I'm in trouble. Miss Fanshaw sent me. I knocked over a bookcase, and I broke a glass jar—"

Mrs Wheeler gave my cousin a considering look. "It's Hannah, isn't it? And you only joined us this term. This doesn't sound like a good start, but I presume it was an accident?"

Hannah nodded furiously. "YES! I mean, yes, Mrs Wheeler. I really REALLY don't know how it happened, and I'm most dreadfully sorry about it—"

"I'm pleased to hear that," Mrs Wheeler told her. "Now, you'd better run along and fetch the caretaker. Phoebe, would you go with her? And Sarah, you can go with—"

CRASH!!!!!!

It was the Merrywood Junior School Sports cup. It had leapt off its stand and hurled itself onto the floor. And as Mrs Wheeler stared, open-mouthed, I tried the Choosing Spell again. For the third time. And under cover of the noise I hissed at Sophie, "Help me! She has to choose Hannah!"

Chapter Ten

It was Vinnie's mention of Special Reading and helpers that had caught my attention. Sometimes I get a feeling that I can't explain – just like I knew that neither Miss Fanshaw nor Josh were making Hannah so unhappy, although they certainly weren't helping. It was more than that. And if I could get my cousin to a reading class, surely someone would notice that something was wrong? So I needed Mrs Wheeler to choose Hannah – but Hannah was the last person she'd pick after what I'd done.

I shut my eyes and tried the spell again, and this time I heard Sophie murmuring

beside me ... then Ava joined in, and
Madison and Lily and Emma ... and then
Melody said, quite clearly, "Come on,
Jackson! We ought to help too!"

Mrs Wheeler looked up. "What was
that, Hannah?"

Hannah looked blank. "Sorry, Mrs
Wheeler?"

Mrs Wheeler put the sports cup back
on its stand. "You offered to help. And
now I come to think about it, that's a
very good idea. You're new here, so I'll
overlook your attempts to break up Miss
Fanshaw's classroom – but don't do it
again. It seems as if a lot of things are
falling about today. You go and help
Vinnie with his reading, and Phoebe and
Sarah can fetch the caretaker." She didn't
notice – or maybe she didn't believe

her eyes – but at that moment two tiny twinkling stars floated down from the ceiling.

I don't know how Mrs Wheeler missed my sigh of relief, it was so loud, but she went back into her office, shutting the door behind her. Vinnie took Hannah's hand. "This way," he said, and began pulling her across the hallway.

"Wait!" Hannah was as white as a sheet. "Vinnie! I can't help you! I ... I'm not good at reading..."

Vinnie gave her a wide grin. "But that's what Special Reading's for, silly! I get it all wrong, but Mr Pole – he helps me. And he says some brains is wired up differently, and THAT'S why the letters get all jumbled up."

Hannah stared at him as if he'd

suddenly sprouted wings and a halo. "WHAT? Do you see letters jumbled too?"

"'Course I do. Come ON!" Vinnie tugged at Hannah's arm. "It's FUN! Mr Pole's the best!" And he towed Hannah away down the corridor. I began to follow them – and that was when I saw Miss Fanshaw coming from the other direction and my heart sank.

"Hannah!" she said sharply. "What are you doing?"

Vinnie looked surprised. "She's coming to Special Reading with me. Mrs Wheeler said."

"Nonsense!" Miss Fanshaw snapped. "Hannah reads beautifully when she tries. Why, when she first got here she dazzled us all!"

Vinnie stared, first at Miss Fanshaw, and then at Hannah. "You told me you saw jumbly letters," he said accusingly. "You told me you weren't no good at reading."

Hannah looked wildly around as if she was hoping to escape. I held my breath.

 105

"Go on, Hannah!" I willed her. "Go on! Tell her! PLEASE tell her!"

"I..." she began, and then she let out a long, long sigh, as if she was letting something go. "Vinnie's right. I'm no good. That book we read – *George's Marvellous Medicine* – I know it by heart. I know lots of things by heart, but I need time to learn them ... it's like Vinnie said. When I try to read I get the letters muddled up."

Miss Fanshaw slowly shook her head. "Well I never. I would never have guessed. What a very clever girl you are, Hannah. Do you really know the whole of *George's Marvellous Medicine* by heart?"

Hannah nodded.

"And you did all the voices, too!" Miss Fanshaw actually smiled. "Well, well.

I know EXACTLY who I want in the next school play! Don't worry! I'll give you lots of time to learn your words ... and Mr Pole will help you too." She gave Hannah an approving nod. "Off you go! Tell Mr Pole that I owe him an apology for not spotting that you had a problem before now. You had me completely

fooled ... well, well. And now I'd better let Mrs Wheeler know you'll be joining the Special Readers' group." And Miss Fanshaw walked away, still shaking her head in astonishment.

I couldn't help thinking that Hannah was owed an apology too, but she didn't seem to mind. She was skipping as she and Vinnie headed across the hall to the classroom opposite, and I heard her laughing at something he said.

"Excellently done," said a booming voice as the Merrywood Junior School Sports Cup flew high in the air and did a celebratory wave before landing back on its plinth. "But we mustn't stay any longer. Time's running out."

As Fairy Prim spoke, the school bell rang to signal the end of break. There

was the sound of hurrying feet, and we had to leap out of the way as the doors swung open and the school poured in. It was hard work fighting our way back to the playground, but Fairy Prim marched in front, and nobody seemed to notice they were being pushed to one side by an invisible presence. I had my feet trodden on, and judging by the muffled squeals so did my friends, but we got out eventually. The playground was empty as we ran to the Travelling Tower and rushed inside – and that was when I began to feel sick. I'd just remembered. We had to make that horrible journey all over again...

Chapter Eleven

Weirdly, it wasn't nearly as bad going back. Fairy Prim called up a Dreaming Spell, so we slept peacefully until the TT arrived back at Stargirl Academy. We woke with a start to find Fairy Prim looking rather ashamed of herself. "Done a bit of damage on landing," she explained. She was right; we could all see the long crack that stretched across one of the Travelling Tower's glass walls. "Never mind. I'll ask Miss Scritch to see to it."

"Can't you do it, Fairy Prim?" I asked, and she shook her head.

"Not one of my strengths." She winked at me. "Besides, think how happy it will

 110

make Miss Scritch." And she laughed her huge booming laugh as the TT door opened wide.

Fairy Mary and Miss Scritch were waiting for us in the sitting-room. The fire was crackling, and it looked wonderfully warm and cosy. Scrabster, Fairy Mary's old dog, was curled up on the rug, and he wagged his tail enthusiastically as we walked in.

"Well?" Fairy Mary looked expectantly at Fairy Prim. "How did our Stargirls get on today?"

Fairy Prim beamed. "I suggest they show you their necklaces."

Of course that had us scrabbling to look … and there they were.

SIX shining stars!

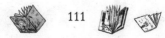

"We've done it!" Madison shouted, and she gave Lily a massive hug. "We've got all six stars! We're Stargirls! PROPER Stargirls!"

Ava was dancing up and down with Emma, and trying to get Sophie to dance too. "Will we have a party?" she asked. "What happens now?"

But I was watching Melody and Jackson. They were looking pleased, but not ecstatic.

"Five," Jackson said quietly. "Five stars."

"Come on, Olivia!" Ava tried to grab my hand. "What's wrong? Don't you realise? We've done it!"

"I think Olivia has something to say," Fairy Mary said. "Am I right, Olivia?"

I swallowed, and nodded. "Yes. Of course I'm pleased to be a proper Stargirl,

but..." I hesitated. What would Team Starlight think of what I was going to say next? "I'm really REALLY sorry, but I don't want to celebrate until Melody and Jackson have their six stars too." I saw Jackson staring, and I made myself go on. "I know they think I'm silly, but they still did everything they could to help Hannah. And besides, we've done

everything together up until now, so it
just seems all wrong to celebrate without
them..." My voice died away.

There was a silence, and then Sophie
came to stand beside me. "I agree with
Olivia," she said.

"Me too," said Emma.

Ava nodded. "And me."

"Me and my big mouth," Madison
groaned. "Of course you're right, Olivia."

Lily sighed. "You're more of a Stargirl
than any of us," she told me. "Isn't she,
Fairy Mary?"

And then the last thing I'd ever EVER
expected happened. Jackson began to cry,
and Melody leapt forward and hugged me.
"We don't deserve you to be nice to us,"
she said. "Not after the things we've done.
But thank you. Thank you very much."

"Melody's right," Jackson sniffed. "Thanks, Olivia."

Fairy Mary smiled. "So are we agreed? We'll celebrate properly when we have EIGHT new Stargirls?"

"Yes," we said.

Jackson pulled out her hankie and blew her nose. "Will Team Starlight be coming

 115

with us on our mission to get our sixth star? Or do we have to go on our own?"

Fairy Mary raised her eyebrows. "What do you think, Team Starlight?"

She hadn't even finished speaking before we'd all agreed. And if the others were anything like me, they were VERY pleased. We'd be back at Stargirl Academy, ready for another adventure ... but there'd be an amazing celebration at the end!

"Then that's settled." Fairy Mary clapped her hands. "And I think you should have a mug of hot chocolate before hometime..."

"No, no! Allow me!" Her sister waved her little silver wand, and at once a tray floated down with eight mugs of steaming hot chocolate. A plate heaped high with marshmallows came next, quickly followed by a small tray of neatly cut cucumber sandwiches.

Miss Scritch gave Fairy Prim an enquiring glance.

"Ahem," Fairy Prim boomed. "There's something I need to confess about the Travelling Tower..."

And Miss Scritch laughed. Actually LAUGHED!

I enjoyed my hot chocolate, but now I knew this wasn't my last time at the Academy, or the last time I'd see my lovely friends, I was dying to get home. What would I find?

When Fairy Mary stood up and opened the door for us, I was the first through – after I'd hugged everybody goodbye, of course. I even hugged Melody and Jackson, and they didn't mind at all.

I thanked Fairy Prim for her help, and

 117

she patted the top of my head. "Well done, Olivia," she said.

Fairy Mary gave her sister a sideways look. "Perhaps if you went to those classes with Olivia's cousin, you might learn how to spell, Prim dearest."

Fairy Prim's laugh sent Scrabster scuttling under a chair. "Rubbish, Mary. Much more fun the way I spell things!" And the last I saw of her, she was labelling the tray, *"Mugs of chocklit. To be woshed!"*

Chapter Twelve

As I stepped out of Stargirl Academy I stepped straight into Hannah's bathroom, and I listened to see if I could hear her crying.

Nothing. No sound at all.

I picked up some tissues, just in case she was crying silently, and made my way to her room. She was sitting at her table, but she jumped up when she saw me. "Olivia! DO sit down! I've absolutely LOADS to tell you. Guess what?"

"What?" I asked, although I hoped I knew already.

"They've discovered I'm... What's the word? Dyslexic! And that's why I've always had trouble reading!" She paused, and looked puzzled. "Did I tell you I had trouble? That I used to HATE school?"

"You might have mentioned it," I said cautiously.

"Oh. I can't remember. But I did

ABSOLUTELY hate it, but yesterday all KINDS of weird things happened, and now I'm having extra help. But that's not the best thing! Best of all is there's going to be a school play, and it's *Alice in Wonderland*, and I'M going to play Alice!"

Hannah was bouncing up and down so wildly that if I hadn't half-guessed what had happened, I'd never have understood what she was talking about.

"And there's this horrible boy called Josh – he used to tease me – but yesterday at lunchtime he actually came and said he was sorry! And Phoebe and Sarah – they're these lovely girls in my class – they said he's never EVER said sorry to anyone before. They said he must fancy me, but I don't think he does, because when Miss Fanshaw asked him if he wanted to be the White Rabbit, he said NO! And then he practically ran away!"

In my mind, I gave Jackson a massive vote of thanks. "I must remember to tell her next time I see her," I thought, and then I felt happy because I was going to see her again. And all my other friends as well...

That night, as I sat in bed reading, I thought how lucky I was. My necklace was beside me, and all six stars were shining brightly – I was a proper Stargirl! But almost better than that was thinking of Hannah, and how she'd waved me goodbye with a massive smile, and how she'd told me she was looking forward to school on Monday.

"Stargirls are the BEST," I said as I

turned out my light and snuggled down.
And as I drifted off to sleep, I thought I
heard wonderful, peaceful music ... the
music Miss Scritch had magicked up
when we arrived at the Academy.

"WOW!" I said dreamily, and shut my
eyes – but not before I'd had one last peek
at my six twinkling stars.

Olivia's Stargirl Crossword

Across

4 What recipe does Fairy Mary give Ava?

6 What does Miss Scritch give to Sophie's little brother?

7 Lily's favourite drink.

8 The name of Little Val and Tallulah's tea shop.

9 What's the name of Sophie's little brother?

10 What's the name of Emma's talkative neighbour?

Down

1 What is Madison's big sister called?

2 What's the name of Olivia's cousin?

3 Lily's favourite phrase.

5 The name of Melody and Jackson's team.

11 Which Stargirl lives with her great-aunt?

Olivia Jones

Good at:
Spelling

Starsign:
Cancer

Hates:
Spiders

Dreams of:
Being more
confident

**Favourite
colour:**
Blue

Loves:
Reading

One Token
www.stargirlacademy.com

One Token
www.stargirlacademy.com

One Token
www.stargirlacademy.com

Collect your FREE Stargirl Academy gifts!

In each Stargirl Academy book you will find three special star tokens that you can exchange for free gifts. Send your tokens in to us today and get your first special gift, or read more Stargirl Academy books, collect more tokens and save up for something different!

3 Tokens — Bookmark

7 Tokens — Star rubber

15 Tokens — Set of star transfers

5 Tokens — Sparkly pencil

13 Tokens — Door hanger

Send your star tokens along with your name and address and the signature of a parent or guardian to:
Stargirl Academy Free Gift, Marketing Department,
Walker Books, 87 Vauxhall Walk, London, SE11 5HJ
Closing date: 31 December 2013

Stargirl Academy

A message from Lily

Jeepers Creepers! Have you read all our adventures? Everything that happened to the six of us in Team Starlight?

Well, I'll tell you a secret. Melody and Jackson have their very own story ... but I can't tell you too much or they'll be FURIOUS. But I can say that it happened at Christmas, and it was VERY exciting...

Stargirl Academy
Melody and Jackson's
Christmas Spell

Lots of love, Lily xxx

PS Don't tell them I told you!